To Steven,
Michael,
and Peter—
May you always find
a friend in one another

Are you my friend?

Janice Derby

Illustrated by
Joy Dunn Keenan

HERALD PRESS
cottdale, Pennsylvania
Waterloo, Ontario

Your skin is rough and wrinkled.
Your hair is white like the snow.
You cannot swing high in the air
or chase a ball,
like I can.
But you can tell me stories
and take me to the park
and talk to me as if I were a grown-up.
Are you my friend?

Your skin is brown like chocolate ice cream,
and sometimes you say words I do not understand.
But when you are sad, you cry,
like I do.
Are you my friend?

Your skin is the color of cream,
  and your eyes are the color of the summer sky.
But you like candy canes, kittens, and kites,
    just like I do.
  Are you my friend?

You have only one leg,
and you sit in a chair with big wheels on it.
But you think butterflies, balloons, and babies are pretty,
just like I do.
Are you my friend?

Cookies
fresh baked

You look like a grown-up and act like a grown-up,
yet you are very short.
But you like airplanes, puppies, and puffy white
clouds, like I do.
Are you my friend?

You cannot see the things I see.
Sometimes you carry a cane
or have a nice dog by your side.
But you like smelling cookies baking
and talking to people who listen to you
and touching soft things,
just like I do.
Are you my friend?

You cannot hear me when I talk to you.
Sometimes you move your hands and fingers
in ways I do not understand.
But you like to read stories
and look at pretty pictures
and go for walks,
like I do.
Are you my friend?

You are older than I,
  yet sometimes you seem younger.
You do not learn things like I do.
  Some things are hard for you to learn.
But when people tease you
  and call you names,
    you feel bad,
      just like I do.
  Are you my friend?

Your skin is tan like the sand on the beach,
  and your eyes are the shape of almonds.
But when you are scared or lonely,
  you like to sit next to someone you love,
    like I do.
  Are you my friend?

Your clothes are old,
  and sometimes they have holes in them.
You do not have money
  to buy candy.
You have only a sandwich
  in your lunchbag.
But you are good at playing hopscotch,
  and you laugh when you have the hiccups,
    and you always share with me.
  Are you my friend?

You are very smart.
You always raise your hand
when the teacher asks a question,
and you always color inside the lines.
But sometimes you ask me
to teach you to skate.
And you like surprises
and silly songs and secrets,
just like I do.
Are you my friend?

You are taller than I.
You can reach the highest shelf
and throw a ball very far.
You are bigger and stronger than I.
But you are afraid of scary movies
and slinky snakes and dark places,
just like I am.
Are you my friend?

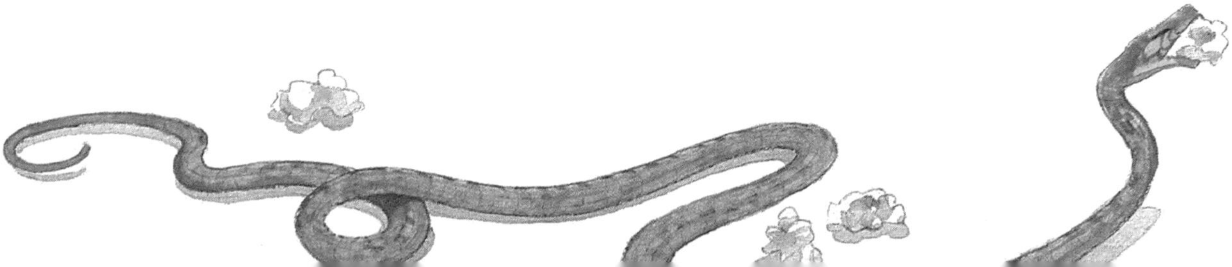

You are smaller than I.
You cannot reach the highest shelf
or throw a ball very far.
And sometimes no one picks you
to be on their team.
But you can jump rope very fast
and draw the prettiest flowers
I've ever seen!
Are you my friend?

You are round and have rosy, chubby cheeks.
You cannot run as fast as I can
or jump as high as I do.
But you like the rain
and roller coasters and riding a bike,
just like I do.
Are you my friend?

Flamethrower

Your skin is dark like the sky at nighttime.
Your hair is black and different from mine.
But you laugh when I do.
Are you my friend?

You are different from me—
but not very different.
I'm so glad we're friends!

Dear Friend,

At school or in a store, have you ever seen people who seemed different from you? Maybe their skin was a color not like yours, or they said words you didn't understand. Perhaps they had only one arm or one leg, or they couldn't see you or hear you. Maybe they just seemed much bigger or smaller than you, or older or younger than you.

There are many people in our world. Every one is different and special in their own way. Our world would be boring if everyone looked the same way and talked the same way and acted the same way.

Sometimes, when you first meet someone who seems different from you, you may wonder why they are different. You may even feel a little afraid. But while on the outside that person may not look like you, inside they are much like you!

You don't need two legs to think butterflies are pretty. You don't need to see cookies baking to like the delicious smell. You don't need a special skin color to feel lonely or sad sometimes. You don't even need to be young to tell wonderful stories or go to the park. Grandmas and grandpas do that all the time!

Are You My Friend? is a story about someone a lot like you. It's about someone who notices differences in other people and wonders if they can still be friends. It's also about someone who notices how much alike people are in ways that are more important than how they look.

Are You My Friend? is about a friend like you.

Your friend,
Janice Derby

Library of Congress Cataloging-in-Publication Data
Derby, Janice, 1945-
Are you my friend? / Janice Derby ; illustrated by Joy Dunn Keenan.
p. cm.
Summary: While searching for a friend, a child notices how much alike people are in other ways that are more important than the way they look.
ISBN 0-8361-3609-8
[1. Individuality—Fiction. 2. Toleration—Fiction. 3. Friendship—Fiction.] I. Keenan, Joy Dunn, 1952- ill. II. Title.
PZ7.D44173Ar 1993
[E]—dc20 92-38779
CIP
AC

The paper used in this publication is recycled and meets the minimum requirements of American National Standard for Information Sciences—Permanence of Paper for Printed Library Materials, ANSI Z39.48-1984.

Published by Herald Press, Scottdale, Pa. 15683
Released simultaneously in Canada by Herald Press, Waterloo, Ont. N2L 6H7.
Library of Congress Catalog Card Number: 92-38779
International Standard Book Number: 0-8361-3609-8
Printed in the United States of America
Book design by Paula M. Johnson

02 01 99 98 97 96 95 94 93 10 9 8 7 6 5 4 3 2 1

'he Author

Janice Derby was born in Vacaville, California. Her interest in writing began as a child and continued into her teen years. She won several local essay and poetry-writing contests and awards. Her stories and poetry have been published in periodicals.

Derby graduated from California State University at Chico with a bachelor of arts degree in English and Spanish. She earned additional teaching credentials and has taught at levels from kindergarten through elementary, middle school, high school, and adult education.

Now Derby teaches Spanish to grades 7-9 and English as a second language in Livermore, California, where she lives with her youngest son, Peter. Her sons Steven and Michael attend universities.

Ideas for her stories come from her experiences as a mother and teacher. She has done volunteer work for the local hospital and for St. Michael's Catholic Church, of which she is a member.

Illustrator

Joy Dunn Keenan wished to grow up, but not old, in a thatched split-level a wee bit to the left of the second star to the right. As such things happen, she has spent all her days just off exit 105 of the Garden State Parkway. But her heartbeats and songs have been overheard in lands that have never known her footprints, in other gardens yet remembered, in other kingdoms yet promised.

Some stumble into Narnia through the back of a wardrobe, others through blank paper on a drawing board. Joy has been a working artist since the age of two, with techniques ranging from crayon on baseboard, to #2 yellow pencil on blue-lined notebook paper, and English watercolors on French paper.

Joy lives at Eatontown, New Jersey, with her husband of seven years (Michael Keenan), thousands of books, dozens of stuffed animals, and one monstrously large somnambulistic kitty. She is a deacon of Hope Presbyterian Church and involved in community service.